I am Life

Written by Elisabeth Helland Larsen
and illustrated by Marine Schneider

Translated from the Norwegian by Rosie Hedger

Published by Little Gestalten, Berlin 2017
ISBN: 978-3-89955-793-0

The German edition is available under ISBN 978-3-89955-792-3.

Typeface: Minion Pro by Adobe
Printed by Nino Druck GmbH, Neustadt/Weinstraße
Made in Germany

For more information, please visit little.gestalten.com.

Bibliographic information published by the Deutsche Nationalbibliothek: The Deutsche Nationalbibliothek lists this publication in the Deutsche Nationalbibliografie; detailed bibliographic data are available online at http://dnb.d-nb.de.

This book was printed on paper certified according to the standards of the FSC®.

I am Life

By Elisabeth Helland Larsen and Marine Schneider

Translated by Rosie Hedger

I am Life.
Just as Death is Death,
I am Life.

It's me who sets
everything in motion.

I plant seeds
and water all
that grows.

I am there in everything that breathes,
and in every creature with a
heart that creates a rhythm of its own.

Hearts that can
drum with fear
or be filled with joy.

Hearts that need
to receive love
in order to give love.

We might meet
for a fleeting moment
or for an eternity.

I fly alongside insects
that live for no longer
than a single hour.

I swim with turtles
that might live
for two hundred years.

I climb with squirrels
in the treetops,
summer, winter and spring.

I place my hand
on every mother's
growing tummy.

I follow children
through to adulthood,
when they have children of their own,
who then have children of their own.

Little and large,
they form lines so long
that they could reach all the way
around the world.

Like strong bonds
in a web formed
over millions of years.

The force that causes
the world to turn
is found in everything
and everyone.

In the bees that
carry pollen
from bloom to bloom.

In the fish that
create waves that
stretch all the way to land.

In all the people
who can see one another
and reach out a hand.

Everyone I meet
has a body of their own.

A body that can taste
snowflakes as they float down
from the sky.

A body that can hear
the hungry pussycat
that wants to come inside.

A body that can see
stars that shine and the moon
becoming a fine line in the sky.

A body that
can shout out loud and
dance whenever it likes.

A body that can create tears
and that knows
its own mind.

A body that can find
another body
to lean on.

HOME
SONJA

A body with wrinkles
that look like a map
of the journey it has taken.

A body with silver hair
and eyes so wise that
there's no need for words.

A body that can see
poetry in raindrops
as they hit the earth.

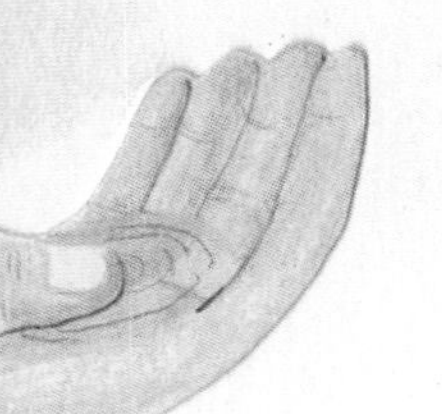

When Death comes,
I'm always there.

We live
on this earth
together.

Many wonder
about the meaning of me.

Some people go parachuting
to feel a fluttering in their tummy
as proof that I am there.

And others are so worried
about meeting me that they
hide in a corner in fear.

Perhaps you often ponder
things that have happened
and things yet to come?

Then it is important
not to forget that I exist,
here and now, inside of you!

The thing I love
most of all
is giving strength and hope.

I can hold you
when you feel remorse
for something that you've done.

I can show you the spring
when you need to see that
something grows.

I can bring peace
to your heart
even if all you may
have seen is war.

I can fill you
with love
even though everyone
you know is gone.

I can walk with
you when you need
to find a new home.

I am always
there with you.

And when you
need it most of all,
I will be there to remind you
just how precious you are.

Because,
in the whole,
wide world,
there is only …

… one of you!

And every day
you can show the world
who you are!